Tom Th
and th
Football
Team

Pippa Goodhart

Illustrated by
Philippe Dupasquier

OXFORD
UNIVERSITY PRESS

OXFORD
UNIVERSITY PRESS

Great Clarendon Street, Oxford, OX2 6DP,
United Kingdom

Oxford University Press is a department of the University of Oxford.
It furthers the University's objective of excellence in research, scholarship,
and education by publishing worldwide. Oxford is a registered trade mark of
Oxford University Press in the UK and in certain other countries

First published in this edition 2016

British Library Cataloguing in Publication Data
Data available

978-0-19-837720-7

7 9 10 8 6

Paper used in the production of this book is a natural, recyclable product
made from wood grown in sustainable forests. The manufacturing process
conforms to the environmental regulations of the country of origin.

Printed in China by Leo Paper Products Ltd.

Acknowledgements
Cover and inside illustrations by Philippe Dupasquier
Inside cover notes written by Sasha Morton

Contents

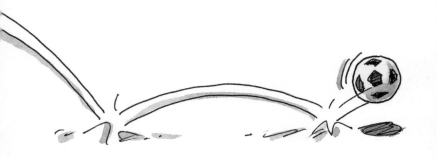

Chapter 1
One Teeny-Tiny Child

There was once a man who loved his wife
and he also loved football.

His wife loved the man and their home.
But what she really wanted was a baby
to love.

She longed for a baby as you or I
might long for a drink on a hot day.

The woman said to her husband, "Just one teeny-tiny child would make me happy."

And, believe it or not, that's exactly what the woman got. She gave birth to a teeny-tiny baby boy.

"We'll call him Tom," said her husband. "Tom Thumb, because he's no bigger than my thumb."

The woman wrapped her teeny-tiny
baby in her best cotton hankie. She cut
the end of the finger from her finest pair
of gloves to make him a little cap. She
tucked Tom into an eggshell cradle and
she was happy.

Well, the years passed as years do.
And Tom's mother did what parents do.
She cooked for Tom and sewed for Tom
and taught Tom to crawl and walk
and talk.

But as Tom grew from being a baby to
being a boy, he grew to want more than
cuddles and pretty clothes and nice food.
He wanted friends and fun. He wanted to
find out about the world.

Chapter 2
Let Me Out!

"I'm bored," said Tom to his mother one
day. He was kicking currants all over the
table.

"Well," said his mother. "If you'll stop
spoiling those currants you can see how
I make a nice pudding for your father's
dinner. Sit on my thimble and watch
what I do."

But there's not much fun to be had in watching a spoon being stirred around above your head. Tom wanted to see how the flour and eggs and milk all mixed together inside the bowl.

So, when his mother turned to boil a pan of water, Tom reached his teeny-tiny hands up to the rim of the mixing bowl.

He pulled and kicked himself up so that he could look down and see and smell the spicy mixture.

"Mmnn, yum!" said Tom. He bent forward to reach a finger to take a taste ... and he toppled over the top of the bowl, plop, into the mix!

If you have ever fallen into an uncooked pudding you will know what sticky stuff it is. It clagged to Tom's arms and clogged to his legs. The more he struggled, the more he got stuck in it.

His mother picked up her spoon and slap-slopped the pudding mix, knocking poor Tom dizzy.

Then she scooped the mix, dollop, drop, plop, into a cloth. She tied it tight and popped it into the water to cook.

The water was hot.

"Yeow!" yelled Tom, and he kicked and he struggled.

At last, Tom's mother noticed that her pudding was jumping around and shouting.

"Well I never!" she cried. "The pudding's alive! Help!"

And she snatched the pudding from the pot and she threw it out of the house and slam-shut the door.

"Ouch!" said Tom as the pudding
landed in the grass. Then "Oooer!"
because somebody had picked the
pudding up.

That somebody was a hungry man
passing by.

"Well, boggle my eyes, a pudding for
free! I'll have that," said the man.

"Put me down!" shouted Tom's teeny-tiny voice. "Let me out!"

"Well, what do you know!" said the man. "The pudding's alive!" And he dropped the pudding and he ran.

Tom bit with his teeth and he kicked
with his feet and picked with his fingers.
He tore through the pudding cloth
and escaped. He wasn't far from the
cottage ... but a cat was sniffing
close by.

Chapter 3
Goal!

"Ma!" shouted Tom, and he ran on his teeny-tiny legs and he kicked the door as hard as he could, bang, bang, bang.

"Open up, Ma!" he shouted. "Quick! There's a cat that likes the smell of me!"

Tom's mother opened the door. She looked in front of her. She looked to the left and to the right.

"There's nobody there!" she said.
But Tom kicked at her ankle.
"It's me, Ma!"

"Well I never, it's my darling boy!" said his mother.

She carried Tom safe inside and she bathed him clean in a teacup. She told Tom, "From now on, my darling, I'll not let you out of my sight."

After that, Tom was kept indoors.
He got more bored than ever.

He climbed the curtains.

"Get down from there or you'll fall!"
said his mother.

He caught a mouse and took it for
walks on a lead.

"That thing could bite you. You can't
keep it," said his mother.

So Tom stood at the window. The children outside were playing football.

"Can't I go out and play with them, Ma?" asked Tom.

"Oo, no, it wouldn't be safe," said his mother.

Tom scowled and kicked the window, boom, boom, on the glass to make his mother as angry as he was.

But one day Tom's dad said to him, "Tell you what, lad, why don't I teach you how to play football like the other children?"

He took a marble from his pocket and he put it, plonk, rumble-roll, on to the table.

"Here, Tom," he said. "Have a kick of this and see if you can get it between those two candlesticks. My fingers will be goalie."

Now, a marble on a polished table is fast. Tom dribbled and darted and dodged and kicked and scored.

"Goal!" he shouted.

"You're good at this!" said
his dad.
They played and played.

"I want to play on a team," said Tom.
"I want to play with the children outside."
"You'll have to ask your mother about
that," said his father.

"Can I, Ma?" asked Tom.

"No, my darling, you cannot."

"Why not?" asked Tom.

"Because," said his mother, "you are teeny-tiny precious. Those other boys might tread on you! No, you stay safe inside with me."

Chapter 4
Oh, Wow!

But one day, Tom's mother was in the
doorway, chatting as parents do.

Tom sneaked out around his mother's
ankles.

But as soon as he got outside,
something strong picked Tom up and
lifted him high into the sky.

Tom struggled and twisted and saw
that he was in the beak of a big black
raven.

"Let go, you bully!" said Tom.

When he looked down he saw his
cottage and his ma shrunk teeny-tiny far
away. And he saw great green mountains
and a big blue sea that he'd never seen
before.

"Oh, wow!" he said.

The raven swooped low as they got to the sea. It opened its beak and dropped Tom. He fell, splash-thrash, into salty cold water.

"Oh no," thought Tom. "I'll drown!"

But, as Tom splutter-splashed, a big fish opened its mouth and gulped. It swallowed Tom right down into its dark, smelly stomach.

"Oh, Ma," thought Tom. "I wish I'd stayed home safe with you!"

He curled up small and cried.

But it wasn't long before a fisherman caught that big, fine fish and he sent the fish to the palace.

The palace cook took one look at the fish and said, "I'll stuff it full of herbs, just as King Arthur likes it." And he took his knife and he slit the fish – and out stepped Tom Thumb, blinking in the light. He pointed at the cook and shouted,

"Put that knife down!"

"Er, yes, Sir," said the cook, and
he put down the knife.

There was a rare fuss-flurry in the
palace as people told each other the story
of Tom Thumb. Even the King got to
hear it.

"I want to see this teeny-tiny boy,"
said the King.

Chapter 5
What's So Funny?

So Tom was brought to the King, freshly washed and combed.

When King Arthur saw teeny-tiny Tom on his table, he began to laugh. So Tom put his teeny-tiny hands on his teeny-tiny hips and asked, "What's so funny?"

"You are," said King Arthur. "I've never seen anything like you before."

"Well, I've never seen anything like you before either!" said Tom. And he pointed at the king and he laughed. "Hee hee hee, look at him!"

The Palace people were shocked.

"Shall we remove this rude boy?" they asked.

King Arthur shook his head.

"No," he said. "Tom Thumb is right.
I am just as much the only king around
here as he is the only teeny-tiny boy.
It can be lonely being the only one.
I could do with a friend who knows how
I feel."

"So could I," said Tom.

So the teeny-tiny boy and the great
grand king became friends.

King Arthur taught Tom how to behave
with dignity. And Tom taught the King
how to have fun. He put a hazelnut on to
the table.

"Flick that with your finger," said Tom.
"See if you can get it past me."

King Arthur got good at dodging and darting.

"It's even more fun with more people," said Tom. "You need two teams to play football properly."

"But where could we get two teams from?" asked King Arthur.

"There's a team where I come from," said Tom.

"Come on, then," said King Arthur. "Let's go and find them."

Chapter 6
Football at the Palace!

So Tom and King Arthur rode over the
mountains and fields to Tom's village.

When Tom's mother opened the cottage
door, she laughed and she cried. She
hugged Tom welcome home and she told
him off for running away.

At last Tom got free and said,
"Ma, this is my friend, King Arthur."

"Lawks, the King!" said Tom's mother,
and she started laughing and crying all
over again.

The village children came to see what
was going on.

Tom told King Arthur, "These are my friends, the team."

"Pleased to meet you," said the King, and the children giggled and bowed and blushed.

"And this," said Tom, "is my dad. He's brilliant at teaching football."

So the grown-ups sat and talked about
the weather and drank tea as grown-ups
do. And Tom told the children all about
the King and the palace and how he came
to be there.

"Oh, wow!" they said.

"Would you like to come and play football at the palace and see it for yourself?" asked Tom.

"Yes, please!" said the children. "You be our captain, Tom."

So they all travelled back to the palace.

Tom's dad taught the palace people how to kick and tackle and dribble and shoot a ball.

Tom's mother had a chat and tea with
the Queen. And Tom took his team down
to the kitchen to see the knife that had cut
him out of the fish.

43

Then it was time for the match.
The shouting and cheering and arguing
were much the same as at any football
match you or I have ever seen. But the
pitch was a big round table and the ball
was a glistening pearl.

"Kids against the King? We'll easily win!" Tom told the children. And they did.

"Hooray!"

"Would you like to play again next Saturday?" asked the King.

"Yes please!"

As they trundled home, Tom's mother said, "You'll never guess what! The Queen has asked me to sew some special little clothes for her baby princess!"

Tom's dad winked at Tom. He said to his wife, "You'll be busy then. You won't want Tom under your feet all day."

"No, I won't," agreed Tom's ma. "You'll just have to go out and play with the others, Tom."

"Thanks, Ma!" said Tom, and he scrambled up on to her shoulder and kissed her.

About the author

The story of Tom Thumb is the oldest story for children that anybody has found written down. It is a story about a tiny boy and the adventures he has. The story has been written down again and again by different people over hundreds of years. Each of those people has made their own small changes.

I've made a change to the story, too. I've added the finger football part. It seems to me that finger football is just the right game for a boy who is no bigger than a man's thumb!